Rush

Of

Many

Waters

Also by Pauly Hart

Novels:
By the Gates of the Garden of Eden
Novellas:
Superior Respondent
Ouesso to Epena
The Book of Lesser Voices
Mountain to Mountain
The Word of Yahweh unto Enoch
Empire of the Dragon
Finance:
The Richest Man In Babylon Continued Stories
Collections:
Sometimes I Write Tiny Stories
Adelphoi
Poetry:
Stupid Mind Tricks
Book of Love and Laughter
The Cross and the Poet
What is Poep?
I Love You More Than a Fox Loves Blueberries
The Night Clerk Held a Broken Pencil
Spontaneous Psalms
Kick the Prick
Exegesis with Co-Authors:
My Flat Earth
Biblical Cosmology, 8+ languages
Translations:
The Testament of Job in Modern English
Children's:
Mathmagician and Other Tales of Awesomeness
Periodicals:
Modern Epistle (1-8)
Microzine (1-5)
Rush of Many Waters (1-20)
With children authors:
Farrell Family Fables
With Co-Author Jennifer Hart:
Adulting: A Daily Guide on Being an Adultier Adult
Audiobooks:
Biblical Cosmology
Superior Respondent

Rush of Many Waters:
Volume Three
By Pauly Hart

Contents

Blood of the Pecos

1

"Hit her again," I said, gripping my beer until the perspiration around the bottle dripped over my fingers to the ground. "Hit her harder."

Drake had been drinking for a couple of hours now and the way things were headed, it was going to either be "jail or ditch," as he liked to say. Hopefully not jail. Jail was the worst. When Sheriff Thomas had been elected, things had calmed down somewhat, but the beat of life had caught up and things had returned back to where they had begun. Except for the Drazi. They were new, and nobody liked them.

"Hit her real hard." I told Drake. "Hit her until she stops puking."

I had seen my first Drazi about a month ago and she had been real pretty. I had been half lit and she had lured me into an alley near the bar and we had started making out. I was glad that I hadn't gone into the bar earlier and started my usual round, because I wouldn't have had such quick reflexes. She had tried biting me on the arm but I had shook her off. Screaming she had fallen to the ground, writhing. It was early on and we didn't know anything about the Drazi then so I tried talking to her and that had been, in retrospect, a huge mistake.

Now, a month later, whenever they came wandering out from the desert, we just killed them. It was no fun sober though. They whined and cried and screamed but, really, if you let them have their way, you'd end up like Chalmers. Near the beginning, Old Sea (as we all called Chalmers) had shacked up with one for about a week. He didn't show up for work, didn't come out to the bar... Just stayed in his house. After four days of that nonsense, Drake and I went over to his house to see if he had picked up that nasty flu that had been going around. He didn't answer the door but *she* did and invited us inside with pleading hands.

We found Old Sea in his bed crying and moaning and the Drazi was trying to get us to fuck her. She was taking off her clothes, whining and everything, thinking that we would do a three-way, but Drake had gotten real mad at her when she didn't answer us about what Old Sea was doing lying on the bed like that and not moving. He was naked and whiter than his sheets and he had bite marks all over him. She didn't even seem to notice he was there, just started taking off her clothes, getting all in the mood or whatever. Drake pushed her up against a wall, real mad like and then she snapped and came for us, all claws and teeth and Drake had killed her with a baseball bat.

And now here I was, in an alley with Drake, commiserating with the devil-woman this savage act. The Drazi seemed to come in packs, or swarms, or litters... Whatever you want to call it. Really beautiful girls that you could smell the sex on. They looked like big city girls with nice faces, but were dressed in hand-me-downs from anywhere and everywhere. Did they raid a Salvation Army Store? The clothes were years out of date and always dirty. But, who cared - they all died the same. Screaming and puking and then eventually turning into a blackened goo that sank into the ground and stank like skunk.

Drake hit her again, this time right in the jaw, and it fell off, clattering.

"Aww fuck this!" He said, and stood up over her and continued with his boot into her skull until she gurgled and stopped moving. Her head sort of exploded and splattered. She quivered once and then disintegrated.

"That'll show her." I said, kinda drunkenly. My vision was still alright but the old lady teddy that she had been wearing was now just a dark blue bulge in a black puddle. It was a perfect time for the sheriff to pull up. Almost like someone had phoned him.

"Cheryl gave me a call." He said as he got out. His big frame made the car creak, sighing relief as he exited. He wasn't overly fat, but he was really tall. Maybe six feet four.

"She said another one came in, trying to stir up trouble." He looked at us, at the black blob, and then back to us.

"But... No more trouble I reckon?" He said more than asked. He walked over to the black blob and pulled out his phone, snapped a couple of pictures then put it away, taking a look at us again.

"You boys been drinkin?" He asked, knowing the answer. Of course this is what a cop is going to ask, after he already knew better enough to ask. Usually you get this question on a DUI, but under the circumstances, it seemed a bit odd. Obviously we had been. I had a bottle in my hand and we were behind the only bar in town.

"Well hell, Jeremy," Drake began, "of course we've been drinking. Whatchu think?" Drake sassed everyone, even his own mother. The Sheriff, whose name was indeed Jeremy Thompson, gave a little chuckle.

"How many is that this week?" I asked.

"Four, if you count the one Jorge' Garcia caught out on his farm near 302. He thinks he knows where they're coming from so I gave one of the Rangers out of Odessa a ring and he wants to try to track 'em down and bury 'em at the source. You fellas wanna ride along?"

This was news. And I thought the Rangers didn't believe any of it. I said so.

"Well yes, and no." Sheriff Thompson said. "Seems they do and don't believe us, even though the tox reports tell 'em they should. They're gonna let one of their boys come along just to humor me."

"Just to humor you?" Drake almost spat.

"Well, Ranger Gibson from Odessa believes me, so that's who's coming." he said, looking us over. "You boys go home and get some rest 'cause we're starting pretty early in the morning."

2

Around seven I pulled into the station. I could see the Ranger and the Sheriff were already waiting. I brought my .38 Smith and Wesson and my .22 mag Winchester Chuckster. Drake was already waiting with his long-term girlfriend Jordan. She was there in full army gear, borrowed from her brother. Drake had his .44 H&K and she had a .20 gauge Browning shotgun.

"Pumped and ready! Let's fuck those fuckers!" she said, then added a "Yehaaa!" She always had a way with words. The Sheriff and Ranger sort of laughed and then we loaded up into the Sheriff's Suburban.

As we drove along, the tension was thicker than a redneck's pride. The Sheriff decided to try to break it.

"Ranger Gibson's been real quiet on this whole thing." Sheriff Thompson said, looking back at us, winking.

"Because none of the good folk of Midland-Odessa want to believe me. And there's no way I would ever talk to the Army boys down in Stockton..." He said sourly. "Look, I believed you when you sent me those pictures. Don't say I've never been on your side." He looked out the window and continued: "Look, whatever we find, we're gonna kill. From everything you've told me and what I've seen, you can't seem to reason with 'em, you can't talk to 'em, and they're just gonna try to kill you. Right?"

"Exactamundo." I said. "They're horrible and wonderful, beautiful and deadly."

Sheriff Thompson laughed. "Somebody's a poet."

"You seen 'em?!" Jordan asked the Ranger, almost jumping into the front seat.

"Woah girl." Drake said, pulling her back. "She's just mad cause one of em tried to do the nasty to me."

"Hell yeah," Jordan said. "Nobody touchin' my man, except me," she said with a pouty lip, leaning back.

"Yeah we took one in to the jail last week," the Sheriff said. "I called our Ranger friend out here to give it a good look-see." The Sheriff laughed. "One look at him, and her clothes were off and she started grinding on the cell bars." He laughed again.

"What did you do with her?" Jeff asked.

"Well, we tried to draw blood for a sample, but the thing got really weird. She started clawing her whole arm open where we had put in the needle." He turned to look at us for effect. "It got real bad after that, we couldn't sedate her... And we had to put her down. There was nothing else to do."

He didn't elaborate. We didn't ask. Real Texas hospitality.

The desert sun was starting to creep higher into the horizon, it was twenty five minutes from Pecos to Mentone and another thirty five to Angeles, up by the New Mexico border... We were heading west, with the sun behind us, out to the Garcia shrimp farm. It might seem weird, growing shrimp in the desert, but the key issue was land... And land was cheap around here. You wouldn't find the Garcia farm on any map, however. Out here, when you bought the land, you never got any of the mineral or water rights. Oh, sure, everyone drilled for oil, but that was only after you had the mineral rights. It was a separate purchase. The proof that everyone drilled for oil was all around you. Hundreds of thousands of pump-jacks littered the horizon. It was all Pecos had come to be known for - Black Texas Tea.

So the Garcia farm ran on stolen water, even though they had drilled the well themselves, they couldn't legally pump from it. That didn't stop them from filling up a thousand and fifty gallons per unit, and making a killing on profit. The Sheriff knew, but since the farm spent their money in Reeves County, he didn't have any problems with it. Reeves was one of those counties out in the panhandle of Texas, where the lines were drawn by a drunk man. We headed west down one of a thousand dirt roads, this one leading to our destination.

The sky was clouding up already behind the never ending sea of pump-jacks. See ya later sun. Late April had that effect on the sky, torrential rains could cause havoc with their flash floods. So far, things looked good - just clouds. We pulled up to one of the shrimp pools and got out. Jorge' and his son, Manuel, were there to greet us. They told the Sheriff where they had found two other "woman" and then they hopped on their little ATV to take us there. Following that thing for what seemed like hours, we came on a pretty large gully that lead down into some caves. Right then, we felt the first drops of rain.

"Lord Almighty. We're gonna get wet," Jordan said. No one else said anything.

We followed Manuel down into the ravine. Jorge' stayed up with the ATV. The click-clack of his Mossberg 30 aught 6 echoed like a corpse knocking on the inside of his coffin. It was slick going, as the rain was merely bouncing off the dust. We scrambled down, gear on our backs and made it to the bottom. Little streams had already begun to form as we reached the mouth of the cave. There were suitcases strewn about and random articles of clothing here and there, and it stank like hell.

"What in tarnation?" the Sheriff said, and made a show of waving the stench away.

"It's coming from the cave," Drake said, echoing all of our thoughts.

"Course it is dummy," Jordan elbowed him in the side, "what else could it be?"

The wind and the rain were picking up but it wasn't stopping the smell. Manuel shouted something to the Ranger who nodded and Manuel started back up the slope.

"He had to go back to his dad!" The Ranger yelled to us. "Something about making sure the shrimp are alright in the rain."

I laughed. That seemed like it would maybe never be a problem, but then I stopped when I realized that they were supposed to be in saltwater, not rainwater.

"Oh." I said. Jordan laughed at me. I don't think anyone else got the logic. She was quick... or I was just slow.

The rain was really coming down and the Ranger put his hand on his holster.

"Well? Are we doing this thing or not? We ain't got much time!" he almost shouted.

"I think we need to come back after the rain!" I said. "It might get too bad to go in!"

The Sheriff chewed the inside of his lip, thinking things over. He spoke as he turned to us.

"Yeah I reckon we ought to come back after... " But he didn't finish his sentence, he was looking behind us.

"Git... Outta... Here!" he said, but it was too late. From over the top of the lip, Jorge' had gone insane. He was racing his ATV down in on us, Manuel holding on for dear life.

"*Inudar! Inudar! Está viniendo!*" he screamed to us in Spanish. Flash flood, and it's coming this way.

We scrambled towards the side of the cave. No one was suicidal enough to go in, it would be a death trap, but we all knew we could out-run it if we got higher than it wanted to go. See, the trick is to find the break in the water. If you're lucky enough to see it before it hits you, you can get away from it and get on a high spot just out of its reach. You couldn't get around it, you couldn't go through it, you couldn't race it, but you could out-think it. The only goal was: "up."

Which is why Jorge' was driving down the canyon instead of the other direction. He had been fortunate enough to see it before it took him out. The only option left to him was to go downhill and then up the next hill, away and out of reach. All this went through my head in maybe one or two seconds as I was scrambling up the side of the hill behind the cave.

I've read enough books to know that they say: "It all happened in slow motion." Well that's complete bullcrap. It all happened fast and hard. The water didn't come down the sides of the canyon as much as jump off like some sort of insane stampede. It was probably going eighty miles an hour and flew at us like God had opened the floodgates over Noah.

The Sheriff, The Ranger, Jordan, and Drake were all ahead of me. Drake and Jordan on the right and the law on the left. Jorge' and his son were rocketing up the far right side on the ATV and I was stuck behind the Sheriff. Seriously, I couldn't have picked a worse person to follow. He was slow for a big fella and took up a lot of room. The water hit my leg and snapped me up like a croc taking down a poodle. I went down.

I don't know how long I held my breath, but it was knocked out of me before I knew enough to appreciate my Navy drowning training. I bumped, hit my knee and I think I cracked a rib before I came on something hard that wouldn't move. It was a hammer on my back. The strength drained out of me. Nothing I did would let me get away and the small amount of air I had was burning in my lungs. I was going to die.

4

I didn't die, obviously. All I did was black out like a sissy. I opened my eyes to Drake hovering over me in the back of Jorge's house, on what must have been his bed. I was out for only a couple of hours, but they must have been action packed 'cause Drake wouldn't stop talking.

I had gone down into the cave alright, just like you probably thought I did. Didn't go very far though, I had gotten hung up on a ledge. Drake kept telling me over and over how lucky I was, how lucky everything was.

"You don't know how lucky you are man!" he said. "You don't know how lucky all of us were!"

"I know, I know." I told him, rolling my eyes. "You keep telling me. What happened next?"

He kinda paused, looking at me with hard eyes, like he was trying to see if I was messing with him.

"Just tell me already." I said deadpan.

"Well, hell man. I don't really know if I can describe it myself. I mean, for real describe it. Kinda like, it was like... Well... It was kinda like hell." He was fidgeting with his hands, so I knew he was having a hard time with it all.

"There was kinda this huge cliff. And you were stuck on the very edge man. The lip. You don't know how lucky you are man. You were stuck on the very lip of the edge of hell man. Hell!" He paused, scrunched up his brow then kept going.

"So... Okay, we get in there when the water is done moving around and we see you stuck like a fish in a net on the edge of this thing. Manuel and Jorge' and everybody was in there and the water had gone down into the hole. But that wasn't the thing man. That wasn't the thing!" He was standing, arms waving.

"There were like, demons or something crawling up the sides man! Like, Succubus Vampire Demons crawling up the rocks to the top! Hundreds of em! And the farther we looked down, the more there were! Dude! I'm telling you! It was a portal to hell!" He waved his arms up in the air like a Sunday morning preacher.

And, as if God decided to emphasize the point right then and there, a huge *KAWHUMP* shook the room.

"What was that?" I yelled, grabbing the sides of the bed.

Drake looked out the window.

"Oh that's The Sheriff, The Ranger, and Jordan. They decided to go back to her place and unload five hundred pounds of Tannerite into the hole… Judging from the explosion, that ought to take care of the problem. I sure hoped it did.

Janitor

The janitor stood over the floor looking down. All was clean, just the way he liked it. His mop, however, was not. Time to fix that. The squeak of his shoes was a whisper of a lover's secret that only spoke to him. In the supply closet were bags of trash to be taken out, along with the cleaning supplies that he used, as well as the ever-trusty mop sink.

The mop sink was good to him. Always taking away the filth that he collected. He was glad of that. Glad of the replenishment of the water. Glad of the drain.

He rung out the mop several times in the down pressure wringer, twisting the mop as he did. He took out the wringer assembly with the mop still inside and placed it gingerly on the floor and dumped the grayish water. He rinsed out the bucket and placed it upside down on the side of the sink and cleaned the mop itself. After all was done, he checked the supplies, and locked the door.

It was 3:08 on the nose. Perfect. Since the time clock ran on fifteen minute spreads, he could clock out now and it would be counted as 3:15. One minute earlier and it would be counted as 3:00. He placed his keys in his pocket and headed towards the door.

But wait. The full bags were still in the supply closet. He would run it out after he clocked out. Nobody looked twice at him. It wasn't that far to the dump. He would just take it out like every other day. A simple man just taking out the trash. Nothing suspicious.

Clocking out, he saw Sylvia. With a shy wave and a smile he left. She wouldn't understand what I do, he reckoned. She was a normal, and they had their own code. No one would understand what it's like to actually make a difference.

He would make a difference. He would get rich.

He walked to his car and drove to the side of the building. He would get in the side door and get the bags. No problems. Click went the key and in he went. Only Glenda the Witch - Head of Nerata Chemicals HR, was standing right there… In his way.

"Excuse me." He muttered, and moved around them.

"Not working off the clock are you?" she asked as he walked by.

"Nah." He lied. "Just forgot something."

"No. Just an employee." She said into the phone as her conversation continued.

So here was a problem. She was standing there, chatting. He needed to move the bags, but she knew he would be off the clock. There was only one thing to do.

He unlocked the door, stood there for two seconds, and closed it again. Pulling his pen from his pocket, he thought it would do the trick.

The Witch was there as he walked back. He held up his pen in the air. "Found it." He said, smiling sheepishly and pushed the crash bar open.

"Have a good night." she said.

"Alright." He replied.

He got into his car and drove away. He would have to come back later for the bags. Like, maybe an hour. No one would go in there. They better not. He had twelve bricks of weed in one of them.

Orbs of the Over

1

The day that color was invented was one of the best days Kliefel had ever been a part of. At least that is what she thought.

"A very fine addition, if I do say so myself." She had remarked, as she looked at her house for the first time in all its brightness and newness. Where it was gray yesterday, today it was vibrant and full of life.

Kliefel's partner Tharknot had not thought much of it at all.

"Whatever you make of anything, it does not matter the color." He had said, with a frown. Of course Tharknot always had a frown. He wouldn't be Tharknot without it.

Kliefel lived in a small lilac house, with a yellow roof. The house was shaped like a small garlic clove, which she thought was just oh so very cute. Tharknot lived next door to her, in a brick. Not a house made out of brick, mind you, but one very large brick. It had taken him years to carve out the rooms inside of it and finally move in.

They had been neighbors since forever. Kliefel had been the second to arrive into the neighborhood, and had not had been introduced to anyone quite yet.

"A very nice day to you good sir." She had remarked, upon seeing Tharknot for the first time.

"Is it?" He had remarked and said nothing else. She had thought that he was a statue at first, in his front yard, for he had not moved an inch. When she had realized that he was not a statue, she had stared at him for a very long time. She had even walked over to him in his own yard and peered at him, nose to nose.

When he had said "Hallo," she fell down promptly, frightened out of her wits. Only when she had regained her composure had she bid him a good day.

He was dressed in a black coat, with a crumpled black top hat and was soaking wet, even though there was not a drop of rain in the sky.

"I am standing on a fountain." He had remarked, and with that, stepped away. A glorious fountain erupted out from underneath him, dancing in the air, the water splashing this way and that.

"Why in the world are you standing on it?" Kliefel had asked.

"It's too happy." He had remarked, stepped back to it, plugging it up once again.

2

Both Kliefel and Tharknot were orb makers. Now an orb, as anyone knows, is just a circle or ball or planet. Not the type of apparition one has when you have a dusty camera. However, neither one of these is what Kliefel nor Tharknot made. They specialized in Siring Orbs, the kind the king used.

They worked in a little shop just down the street from where they lived. On the same block were five more people, who also worked in the little shop down the street. There was Offie and Slamber, who lived directly across from her, Meemoo and Ocrsnart who lived next to Tharknot. On the other side of all of that was the shop and the offices and the living quarters of Toffee. Toffee was not only their neighbor, but their boss and friend as well.

Early in the mornings they would all come out of their homes, greet each other, and walk down the street to work.

"Isn't it a good day?" Kliefel would ask.

"Terrible." Tharknot would say.

"Wonderful," Offie would offer.

"Rotten." Slamber would pronounce.

"Beautiful." Meemoo would declare.

"Hazardous." Ocrsnart would snarl.

"Well I think some people got up on the wrong side of the bed." Kliefel admonished the group.

"I don't even have a bed," said Tharknot, but before they could even ask him about that Toffee opened the door to the shop.

"GOOD MORNING!" Toffee shouted loudly. Meemoo's long pink hair wisped up into a whirlwind and landed back onto her head sideways. Toffee always said things loudly.

"Good morning Toffee." They all said together, and went inside for their day of work.

3

They all had benches and tables and chairs where they worked. On each bench, and around them, in every bookcase, and nook and cranny were hundreds of thousands of ingredients. Some of the ingredients were harmless, some were explosive and some of them would just turn things upside down. There were Jumpstaloopkins and Posderluffs, Fixamiddles and Turnobens. There were too many to list here. Let's just imagine that whatever you could imagine that they had, they certainly had one of those, and also one with wings.

Kliefel and Tharknot sat at the far end on the left. In much the same direction as their houses were arranged, except that Tharknot sat across from her and not to her right. They were responsible for creating orbs of fixation, fascination and fun, the orbs of siring, all for the King.

The King was a great king, he had created the village and the towers and the castle that sat on the hill above the town. He was just and kind and good and everyone loved him, even grumpy old Tharknot.

Kliefel set about her work with an enthusiasm one usually reserves for the consumption of sugar products. Even though she had only worked there for three weeks, as had they all, she knew exactly what to do and where to put things and arrange them. They knew how to mix them, squash them, sprinkle them and blend them into whatever beautiful creation that she had come up with for that day.

Today she was going to create a masterpiece. Each day she created masterpieces and today was going to be no exception.

With a little Farfendust, a dash of Tulipnose and a pinch of Pocketfeffer, she began to mold a tiny little insect. Something she would call a Zimmsniffer or, an Ant. She hadn't made up her mind just yet. She didn't want to get ahead of herself. It was very pretty and very small. It was purple with yellow stripes, had orange wings and thirteen legs. Tharknot told her that the extra leg would just get in the way, so she changed it to twelve legs. Plus, he thought that she had added too much Pocketfeffer into the mix but she didn't listen to him.

After she was done with her creation, it was Tharknot's turn to add his part to the orb. He created things that were not so happy but very interesting all the same.

He took some Muddlefuss, some Birchtoad and a tiny bit of Jellyswamp and mixed it together with a large hammer. *Stomp! Wham! Splat!* He looked at it and he was very happy... If Tharknot could ever be called happy that is.

What he had made was a Puce Leviathan. He said it very slowly so that Kliefel would not mispronounce it. *Le-vi-a-than.* Whatever it was, it was terribly large and scaly and had fire that came out of his nose when he hiccupped. It was long and skinny, a dark purple color with twelve wings. He had wanted to add a thirteenth wing but Kliefel thought it would just get in the way.

They finished both creations, packed them inside of an orb and sent it over to Toffee for inspection.

They both hoped he liked it.

Toffee had at first loved their idea of the leviathan and the ant, then thought better of it and decided to send it to quality control first. Quality control consisted of two little people who lived and worked in the side of the shop to the left down the hall. Their names were Hopoo and Grek. Hopoo and Grek were gnomes you see. Hopoo and Grek each were around twelve and a half centimeters tall. If you happen to the imperial unit of measurement, that comes to exactly 4.92126 inches. They were both very energetic, always happy and always bouncing and hopping everywhere they went.

They were happy gnomes, for all gnomes are always happy in the great kingdom. Hopoo was blue and Grek was smirt. I'll bet you expected me to say that Grek was green didn't you? But you must remember that color had only recently been invented and not everyone had it down just quite yet. Smirt was kind of green, but not sticky enough.

Hopoo and Grek decided that there was too much Muddlefuss in the mixture and took a little out and put in some Pinkydie. You only used that much Muddlefuss when you wanted something to float really high. But it didn't need to float. After they removed it they happily bounced over to Toffee with the orb.

Toffee had been cleaning out his ear and didn't hear them. This was usually something Toffee did at home for he had very large ears and it took a very long time. This morning he had an especially itchy ear, so while Hopoo and Grek were inspecting the Orb, he had pulled out his scratchy-stick and had begun to rub at them fiercely.

Perhaps Hopoo and Grek should have said something or flashed the lights or waved a flag, because Toffee bumped the orb out of their hands and it sailed out the window onto the lawn. Hopoo had opened the windows earlier because sometimes Grek had problems digesting his legumes.

This was terrible news indeed. Orbs were very fragile when it came to fufflegrass. And the lawn was just silly with it. The Nervipettles and Twitchypads jumped back and the orb landed on a fresh patch of Fufflegrass and with a *FLOOSH* it plished, ploshed and popped open, immediately coming to life.

"*RRAAAAAARRWWWWW!*" said the leviathan with a terrible roar. Then he hiccupped and a bright orange burst of flame came fooshing out his nose and lit the workshop roof on fire. This made him incredibly embarrassed. Now just being born into the world he didn't want his first act as a leviathan to be embarrassing, so he laughed and said: "Ha Ha silly roof! Now you're on fire!" He then spread his terrifically large wings with a snap and flew away. The ant looked at him, and then at the roof and decided that it was better off if it just dug a hole in the ground and hid.

All at once Kliefel, Tharknot, Offie, Slamber, Meemoo, Orcsnart, Toffee, Hoppo and Grek came running out and tumbled onto the lawn in a big pile.

"Look there!" Kliefel yelled, pointing upwards. But no one saw anything, because before they could look, the leviathan was gone.

"Get off of me! I think you're squishing my spleen!" someone hollered.

"Why are you hollering at me?" Offie exclaimed to Orcsnart.

"I thought Grek was yelling at Tharknot!" Orcsnart retorted.

"I'm not blabbering about anyone's spleen." Tharknot blabbered.

One by one they all discombobulated themselves from one another and stood up and looked around. Who had been on top of whom and who had incurred the ever so dastardly spleen injury.

Meemoo, who squirmed out from the bottom of the pile last, looked around. "Who has the squished spleen?"

"I never said I have one." A voice said. "I merely said that I think you were squishing it."

They all looked down to the ground. There, on top of Meemoo's right big toe, was the ant.

The ant was terribly uncomfortably with this. At first he had been frightened of the entire situation. All he had wanted to do was to burrow itself into a nice little hole in the ground. But as it was digging, it realized that in order to be a brave ant, you must first face your fears and deal with them. So it crawled onto Meemoo's toe to do just that.

"Excuse me!" The ant called up to them. They all crouched down and looked at him.

Orcsnart said to him: "What do you want, little bug?" This was strange indeed, for up until now, the word 'bug' had never been used except in case of very odd behaving computer programs. We won't actually get into that now. You see, computers had not been invented yet.

"It seems to me that your roof is on fire!" He said in his loudest ant voice. The others promptly agreed with him. "And I think that we had better put it out, before the rest of the neighborhood goes with it."

Hoppo and Grek were shocked and slightly embarrassed that they hadn't thought of this immediately and were set into motion with these remarks and Toffee led the brigade. "Quick!" he shouted, "Everyone to Tharknot's fountain! Grab as much water as you can!"

And off they went. Throwing themselves into the fountain, everyone got the largest mouthful of water and ran back over and spat on the roof with great gusto. It didn't seem to do anything, because the roof was still alight. It had even seemed to have gotten larger.

"We need to put the water into containers!" Kliefel shouted. In their enthusiasm, they had forgotten that they had a better solution than to just gulp up all of the water in their mouths. In retrospect, it had been a silly idea from the get-go, but no one had done anything differently... Well... You read that already. It was silly wasn't it?

So, into Kliefel's kitchen they went, and got large saucers and gravy boats and shoes and upside down umbrellas and in Slambers case - a sea shell. They ran back to the fountain, filled them up and threw all the water onto the roof.

It sizzled and spattered and eventually was put out. "Whew!" said Meemoo, "That was close." Then they all went into the workshop to see what damage had been done.

6

Miraculously, there was no damage whatsoever to the inside of the workshop. Toffee was extremely glad about this and told everyone that before any work could get done, they should repair the roof.

Out they went. Kliefel, Tharknot, Offie, Slamber, Meemoo, Orcsnart, Toffee, Hoppo and Grek came bouncing, prancing and running outside and scrambled up to the roof. To their surprise, there were a hundred or maybe even more ants all working on the roof. They had pulled off the burned parts, and gotten new supplies and had just finished repairs. They were even drinking tiny glasses of lemonade.

An elderly ant came up to them. He had a long white beard and a cane. "Hello again!" he said. This confused everyone. And I am sure that you can imagine that it would confuse you too. Up on top of a roof and you find yourself talking to an ant with a beard and a cane, drinking lemonade.

"Who are you?" They all asked together.

"I'm the ant that you made. Since you've been gone, I went and made a family. And then they went and made their families and now we see that you've finally put the roof out, so we decided to go get some materials and fix it for you."

Toffee was very relieved and also very puzzled. "But we were only gone a minute! How did you get so old, so quickly?"

Ant time is very different than regular time. And the ant just winked at them, gave a friendly wave of one of his hands and crawled away, back to the ant hill - which was now almost as tall as the workshop itself.

Offie scratched his head. Hoppo and Grek looked at each other. Finally, Tharknot looked at Kliefel and said: "I told you there was too much Pocketfeffer."

It was a busy day, and they decided to go home. Toffee locked the shop and they all headed over to Tharknot's house to see if they could help him finish building his home.

No one ever saw the leviathan again.

Poems

Jesus Christ, Savior Messiah.
You are my everlasting friend.
Be with me now both here and forever.
Be with me unto life's bitter end.
I know that you never will give up on me.
I know that you never will forsake.
Give me the strength to know your love.
Help me for the gospels sake.
Your Word stands strong above the hills.
The mountains shout eternally.
Everlasting heart felt kinship.
The joy this prisoner saw in thee.
I shout your song above the earth.
I sing your song beneath the sea.
Heaven and Earth shall now bear witness.
I in You and You in Me.

Mind set yet

Tenacity, or maybe audacity
perforates this earthly suit
I strive whole-heartedly towards
a Christ-like mind set yet

Why do I strive except
for my own selfish desire
And why do I desire it
To be the best "me" possible

But Jesus doesn't want "ME"
He just WANTS...
And it is an infidel,

Who tries to outguess God.

my brother

someone once bet
my brother
a ton of
potatoes
if i would come
to his wedding

so

when i arrive
my brother
will open
a grocery store

Nothing

Pretense meant nothing to me
when I looked into her eyes
Gazing into coolness
matching spy for spy

She read my like a Bible
Chapter, book, and verse
All the words dried on my tongue
all the lines rehearsed

Pretense meant nothing
as I looked into her eyes
All I could do was think of love
and moments passed us by

Intention

Oh well, I tried not,
   to fight the claim of my election.
Somehow passing life,
   and took rejection.
trudging through the dark,
   and found illusion.
I was all but dead,
   but I claimed protection.
He took my life,
   and gave me redemption.

Privilege

And as many as cast him down

He shall rise to face again

Though many cast him down

He takes on all mighty blows

For as many as cast him down

He will rise to come again

Save one who casts him down

and that one who lives inside

For when that one casts him down

He shall lay prostrate on the ground

> ```
> God is he
> ```

God is faithful
God is just
God is whom
Do I place my trust
God is he
To us be shown
God is God
And God alone
But if I leave
To him not cleave
He will not say
You will bereave
God is faithful
God is just
In him I place
All of my trust

> ```
> Hi, call me trampled
> ```

I saw her sitting
Hiding softly behind her book
Her big brown eyes fluttered
Looking my way

Last night she was with him

The one they call Nick
With her promises broken
She looks away

Spontaneous Psalm #10

Worship you Almighty God
For you're more than just holy
You are almighty

I'll worship you for who you are
Cause you're more than holy
More than almighty and I
Worship you God

And I'll not pain in my anguish Lord
Worship you alone
And I'll not pain in my trials
Give you everything

Essays

Raised on a Pew

Sunday Morning, Sunday Night, Wednesday Night, Tuesday Night Prayer and sometimes Revival Services on Friday... Every single time the door was open we were there. It was ok. It wasn't my first choice, but it did give me a chance to draw and create massive fantasy wars on various tithing envelopes. The Spider Tank People versus the Backpack Helicopter People was always a favorite. That is, until the Spider Tanks became inventive and developed surface to air missiles. Then the Backpack Helicopter people usually bit the dust. But I digress. What I was interested in was space. Lasers, rockets, extra-terrestrials (that's what we called aliens back then,) and a whole bunch of craziness that no one had invented yet. That's what I wanted. That's what I needed. That's what my mind was set on, until I heard a preacher talk about going to heaven.

Roberts Liardon came and preached at our church. He was a nineteen year old kid from Tulsa, Oklahoma and he was on a travelling circuit talking about a book he wrote that explained a trip into heaven. "I saw Heaven" was its name and it simply blew me away. Here he was, only six years older than I was, and he had already been to heaven? Now this was something worth paying attention to. This wasn't some (what I considered at the time) some pansy story about some lady who was bleeding and she got healed. In my estimation of the limits of the power of God, that was like Bones giving Captain Kirk a hypo-spray on his arm after he just got done killing a whole legion of monsters with tridents. "Tell me more about the cool stuff," I cried!

And so, for the next two hours Roberts told his story. I had never listened so intently in church as I had that day. It was better than any sermon I had ever heard. It recounted his travel in the spirit realm to heaven and how he walked around with Jesus and did fun cool stuff. Today, I don't remember much of it, and I couldn't tell you if any of it was true or not but it changed my mind from: "Church is dumb." to "Sometimes if you look deeper, God will surprise you." And that's what I came away with. I called it "Phase Two" in my head and started looking for it everywhere I went. Well, everywhere in one church that is. I really didn't "pick up the bible and read it for myself" all the time just yet but I would start studying the scriptures that were being preached at the pulpit... That was new... Or something like new. I had opened up my mind recently to the Holy Spirit when I had become baptized and now his words were becoming real to me as well. More seeking and more questions began to open up to me.

Now, honestly, I haven't really kept track of Roberts Liardon recently and I don't honestly even know what he's all about, but the point is that I experienced something in his testimony that wasn't dry and crusty and stuffy religiosity. I saw something alive and active and real. Really real. The kind of God that the children of Israel must have encountered when Moses came down off of the mountain and they couldn't even look at his face. The God who lived inside of a huge pillar of fire that rested on the dome of the tabernacle. A living god above all thought or imagination. A god of gods. A reality changer. An intelligent designer. As Abraham called him: "God Most High." This is who I saw in the preaching and this is who I sought after.

The Roberts Liardon Equation

So the real story of me begins with me. Who I am was a little blend of all the people before me, all the way back to my Hebrew roots of Noah... But the reality of my makeup was consistent with the Intelligent Designers plans for me. As a person who appreciates a well-designed plan, I realized that I should lean towards the idea that God had a purpose for me when I was created... Flaws and all.

After leaving Indonesia, my father's company, moved us to Denver, Colorado, where we attended a wonderful place called: "Happy Church." My mother and the Pastor's wife, Marilyn Hickey, hit it off due to their love of Spanish. My mother, having Spanish as her first language, aced college with a Masters in Spanish and a minor in teaching. Marilyn's focus had been the same. Also, because of my childhood ailment, "Prune belly syndrome," I had fallen victim to heart issues, something that Marilyn had been healed of as a child. Their friendship was a bond. Together, Mary Smith, Marilyn Hickey, and my mom, Kay Hart, would be a tight clique of besties.

One fine day, on a lazy Sunday morning, Marilyn's husband, Wally was giving an inspiring sermon about how Jesus had come to save humanity. At the eager age of four, I was on the edge of my seat. In mid-sermon, I ran down the center aisle of the church and said: "Who is this Jesus? I want Him in my heart right now!" I ran up the steps to the podium and Wally Hickey and the whole of the church were laughing. Not laughing at me, but at the whole scene where the little boy who so desperately needed Jesus in his heart runs down an aisle to get to him. My parents appeared and Wally Hickey shooed them off. He put me on his shoulders and used me for the altar call right then and there.

When we moved to Wichita, Kansas it was again at the behest of my father's company. We found a little church and went there twice on Sunday and once on Thursday night for Bible Study. We went for the special functions and tent revivals and went when Robert Tilton had his special satellite telecast. Years later, I've tried to stay in touch with the church staff, but they've rebuffed my attempts. The Pastors all rebuffed me. It was especially hard when one of the staff passed away in 2018, as I still attempt to make amends with these fine folks. For it was at that little church that I encountered the real and living God in various signs, wonders, and miracles.

I could probably write a book and expound on all of these, but here in this article I will focus on one. It was probably 1984 when Roberts Liardon and his buddy Rudy visited the church. They called people up to the front to lay hands on them and have them expect a miracle. I was still a sickly child at thirteen years of age, still suffering from various issues of Prune Belly Syndrome. I had a heart murmur, swayback, stomach, intestine, kidney and liver issues, and several related to the reproductive system. At least I didn't have to wear my girdle and leg braces any more. Those had been so embarrassing.

Roberts and Rudy had us all line up and laid his hands upon us, going down the "Charismatic Healing Line" as it was called. James five speaks of this idea: "Is any sick among you? Let him call for the elders of the church; and let them pray over him, anointing him with oil in the name of the Lord: And the prayer of faith shall save the sick, and the Lord shall raise him up; and if he have committed sins, they shall be forgiven him." And so with that verse in mind, he laid hands upon me. I fully expected a miracle or something. I need to be healed. I shouldn't have even survived as long as I had, to tell you the truth. Doctors still wondered why I was alive.

Roberts was seated, having prayed over several people, and Rudy prayed over the remainder. Rudy moved down the line one person after another. He didn't pray for me, but prayed for the person to my left and to my right. My mother had come with me and stood behind me. She was 5'9", a good three inches taller than me. I looked up at her and wondered why nothing had happened. I hadn't even felt anything like a tangible anointing come over me. Often, when one is prayed for, the expectation arises and people fall over being "Slain in the Spirit." That was not the case with me. I didn't let emotions overrule my body in such a manner... I rarely "Fell Out" in meetings.

When all had been prayed for, Rudy walked passed me again. Then he walked by again. Why was God ignoring me? I was the only one still standing up. I tried to be super-religious and close my eyes and raise my hands in surrender, until I realized that he was in front of me again.
"Is this your mother?" He asked.

"Yes."

"Is your father also here?" He asked.

My dad stood up from the pew.

"Dad, why don't you come on up?" Rudy said to my father.

He had them stand on the left and right of me, holding my shoulders and arms.

"Now, I haven't obeyed the Lord yet..." Rudy began, "I've been asking Him to be real specific with me about what I should do, but I can't get away from the idea that I need to pray for your back."

I nodded.

He looked at my parents. "I need to pray forcefully over his back. Is that okay with you?"

They both nodded.

"I need to punch him in the back. It won't hurt him, it will heal him. But this is what the Lord wants me to do, and I would like your permission." Rudy said to them.

It was just right exactly then that all four of us felt what seemed like a blanket made of honey descend on all of us, making our lips and noses an d fingertips go numb. My parents were both in tears. I was in tears. It was the Holy Spirit of God.

"Thank you Lord. Thank you precious Holy Spirit." Rudy said.
Rudy then calmly walked behind me and punched me in the back.
"Be healed in the name of Jesus of Nazareth!" He cried out with all his might.

I crumpled like a wet paper bag.

Maybe five minutes later I got up and looked my mother in the eye. Mind you, I didn't look up at her. I looked her straight on. She wasn't taller than I was anymore. In the span of five minutes, I had grown three inches. My pants were showing my socks, but I wasn't wearing hi-waters moments ago. My mom was in shock. My dad checked my spine. Where the large bend to the left and right had been, was now a straight back. I was healed. Miraculously, spontaneously, and perfectly healed.

How a vagabond lifestyle has built my inner person

My friend Kevin used to call them: "Urban Outdoorsman." You know, the men and women living under the bridge with their shabby clothes and their blue tarp blowing in the wind. The homeless. The seeming unwanted citizens of our great land, stuck down by a financial blow. What brought them to this low position? Was it debt? Lifestyle? Calamity? Who knows their story better than they do. I only know of one story, and that's mine.

Today I sit in my air conditioned home with my two cats lazily sprawled out by my feet. It was a hard road to get here, and I think that it would be insane to do it all again, but I know that if it ever came to it, I would know how to do it again, if necessary. The funny thing is, if it actually did happen again, it would be the sixth time. Wow, six times. Even hearing it now brings a shake to my head, yet, it's the truth. I have been homeless and jobless six times. But I bounced back every time. And here I am today... Cats included.

The first time it happened I was a student in college. Shirking the dorms and choosing an apartment lifestyle had its perks and it was the path I chose. Roommates came and went and after three years, most everything in the unit was mine. The program I was in was quickly coming to an end so I was looking to liquidate all of my belongings because, well, it was just *stuff* and I was rather fed up with it all. I liked my freedom and I didn't want to be bogged down. So I gave it all away to a needy man who had just undergone a house fire. I didn't think anything of it. I was 21 and life couldn't stop me.

Lesson #1 – Reciprocity (or Karma) is your bedrock.

Until the week that I was moving... And everything fell apart. Fortunately, I had parents to fall back on. I crashed with them, found a job at Kentucky Fried Chicken, and moved out once I had money. It was quick and painless but at the time it was the real deal. But it was nothing like the next time it happened. After about a year of living on my own, I got a job at a summer camp in another state, for next to nothing. I had attended this camp as a child so I sold everything I had and drove up there on a whim and a prayer and had a fantastic summer. But as soon as summer camp was over, I had nowhere to go, and, as luck would have it, my car died. So, I sold it and hitched a ride to my old church with the hopes of working there. And that panned out fine. The church was impressed that I had worked at the camp and offered me a job with a neighboring ministry.

Lesson #2 - Following your small dreams will lead you closer to your big dreams.

And so, things were great until I found out that my mother had become ill. I quit my job, packed all my things up in my car and headed home – Again, no job, no home. Fortunately, my parents (ever loving) allowed me to stay with them once again. It was a hard time. My mother eventually passed away and I moved out into another apartment. I had acquired a job as a youth minister with a church. It was only part time, so, during nights, I was a DJ at a dance club. Things were great. Life was great. And then I met "the girl of my dreams" and yes, you guessed it... I gave away all I had and moved with her to another state. Except this time, I totaled my car on the way. And with two suitcases I moved in with who I thought was to be my soul mate forever and ever.

Lesson #3 – Attaching yourself to others means you are letting go of yourself.

Fast forward four years. We own two cars, a small coffee-shop, a house with a white picket fence, a black Labrador and have plenty of friends and family. Until she told me that she was pregnant with her boyfriend's baby. Needless to say, everything fell apart. In eight months I had lost everything. I had been divorced, robbed, burglered, totaled one car, had another stolen, closed the business and the dog ran away. It was the worst country music song ever. With eviction notice in hand, I remember sitting alone on Christmas in my vacant tiny apartment after the gas had been shut off. "How had it all come to this?" I thought. Then the phone rang. Jason, my friend from the camp I worked at years before, told me that he had a dream about me, and that he was coming to pick me up to move in with him.

Lesson #4 – Opportunity doesn't always knock. Sometimes it uses a battering ram.

Months after I moved in with Jason I met another girl. No. It's not what you think. We divorced soon after, but today I am home with my third wife. She's wonderful and our cats love the air conditioning. I've given my life and possessions away three times now and do not regret it. I've owned 28 vehicles, six of which I have given away. It's allowed me to build somewhat of a spiritual bank account. I now am blessed with a woman who loves me for who I am, and am one of the happiest people that I know.

My wife and I just bought a school bus that we are renovating. We will be moving into it full time next year. Next month we will be selling most of the things in our home and getting ready for another chapter in our lives. It's going to be small and uncomfortable at first, and to be honest it's going to be a lot harder on her than it will be on me, but that leads me to lesson number five.

Lesson #5 – Never give up on what you really want to do.

Best of luck!

www.ingramcontent.com/pod-product-compliance
Lightning Source LLC
Chambersburg PA
CBHW051929220626
47052CB00003B/632